I0698883

The Coach Café
(In Quest of Purpose)

Roxanne R Vasquez

Disclaimer

The author and publisher do not assume and hereby disclaim any liability to any party for any loss, damage, or disruption caused by errors or omissions, whether such errors or omissions result from negligence, accident, or any other cause. The names, characters, businesses, places, events, and incidents are either the products of the author's imagination or used in a fictitious manner. Any resemblance to actual persons, living or dead, or actual events is purely coincidental.
This book is not intended as a substitute for the medical advice of physicians, nor for the legal or financial advice of concerned experts.

Book Writing Consultant

Printed in the United States of America
Page Trim Size: 6 x 9 inch
Typeface: Garamond

First Edition: 2025
ISBN (Paperback):   978-1-970846-12-6
ISBN (Hardcover):   978-1-970846-13-3

DEDICATION
& ACKNOWLEDGEMENTS

A heartfelt thanks—

To my husband, Larry, for bringing me to Seattle
and always sweeping me off my feet with his crazy,
beautiful family dreams.

To my firstborn, Trisha, for opening my mind and
helping me appreciate new things about her
millennial world.

To my youngest, Zach, for driving me around town
and always protecting and supporting me like a
tireless bodyguard.

To my Mom and Dad in Heaven, who may not be
here anymore, but whose memories of love and
guidance see me through.

To family and friends,
to whom I always run when I need a quiet space.

And to all the readers who will give this book a
chance—

May you always live inspired.

TABLE OF CONTENTS

Preface

MARIA LEMAIRE is a woman blessed with warmth, selfless dedication, and an unwavering passion for service. Yet, a tragic mishap shattered her sense of identity, leaving her uncertain of who she truly was or what she wanted from life.

At Café de Amor, she found herself connecting effortlessly with people who were naturally drawn to her gift for listening and offering guidance. Over time, she became affectionately known as "The Coffee Coach," a beacon of hope and inspiration to everyone she touched.

In a heartwarming twist, as Maria helped others navigate their struggles, they, in turn, guided her back to the world she had lost—her home, her purpose, and her true calling.

The Coach Café invites readers into meaningful conversations about life, purpose, and transformation. It is more than a story to be enjoyed; it is a gentle companion that encourages reflection and inspires readers to apply its lessons to their own personal journeys.

Ricardo and His Pocket of Hope

"So… what do you want to talk about today, Ricardo?" Maria asked gently as she settled into her chair.

"Thanks for taking the time to see me, Maria," Ricardo mumbled. "I've been coming to you for so long now, and I just can't quit this frustrating habit. I'm so sorry, but…"

"Shush, Ricardo," Maria hushed him softly. "This is your personal space. You apologize to no one."

"But it's been years. Oh no, mi amiga… I've just been wasting your time," Ricardo muttered, shaking his head.

"No, Ricardo. This is about you—for you. Every time we share coffee together, remember this is precious time for you to listen and talk to yourself. When you hurt, feel it. If you need to forgive, then you have to." She smiled warmly. "Be patient with yourself. Only when you fully understand where you stumbled can you start again. So… why don't we do that now? Start again. For you, mi amigo."

Maria's smile brightened—the very smile that drew so many client-friends to her corner at Café de Amor.

Ricardo took a slow sip of his hot Americano and paused, gathering his thoughts.

"Maria… I'm ashamed to admit this. I had another bottle of vodka last night," he confessed, bowing his head, his voice thick with shame and frustration.

"Then you must have a terrible headache today. Are you sure you're up to talking? We can meet tomorrow if you need to rest," Maria offered gently.

"I need this coffee anyway. Let's get this through," Ricardo said, his tone resolute.

"Okay, then. Tell me, my friend. What happened? You've been sober for months. You were doing great. Why do you think you slipped again?" she asked, her voice calm but probing.

"I saw her with him, Maria. I saw Leila, my dearest, with her new man."

He raised his cup for a gulp, but Maria stopped him. "Careful—it's still hot," she warned kindly.

He sighed heavily. "I couldn't get her sight out of my mind all night. Oh, you should have seen her, Maria. She looked… so happy. She's certainly moved on without me."

Maria noticed the tears forming in his eyes. He was fighting them back, but she could sense the dam about to break.

"And everything came back!" Ricardo suddenly shouted, pounding both hands on the table.

Then, in a cracked whisper: "The betrayal. All the rage came back. What a pathetic loser I've become…"

Finally, Ricardo broke down. He covered his face, shoulders trembling, as if trying to rub the memory out of his mind.

From across the room, Lamberto Amore, the owner of Café de Amor, glanced over with concern. Maria gave him a discreet thumbs-up—she was still in control.

She stayed silent, letting Ricardo cry it out. Maria had built what her client-friends called their "safe personal space"—a gift that made her known as "The Coffee Coach." It was why so many regulars came here not just for the coffee, but for her presence.

When his sobs subsided, she finally spoke.

"Ricardo… you know alcohol is restricted for you now. It will harm your body more than help. For almost a year, you've been protecting yourself from further damage. Tell me honestly—did the vodka help at all?"

"It made me forget, for a few groggy hours," he admitted with a half-chuckle. "But now I've got this awful headache."

"We've talked many times about what happened between you and Leila," Maria reminded him gently.

"Yes… I know. I've forgiven myself. And her, too," Ricardo replied, then went quiet, lost in thought.

Maria didn't interrupt. She knew he needed this pause to gather himself. As a skilled coach, Maria understood her role was to guide Ricardo toward seeing his situation with absolute clarity before taking action. She listened intently, giving him the space to reflect on his past, knowing that this silence was a vital part of the coaching process, allowing him to uncover insights on his own.

Ricardo had divorced Leila more than three years ago. They never had children, though he had been a good provider during their marriage. But his heavy drinking slowly eroded their bond. Night after night, he stopped at bars to "unwind," until stress became an excuse and alcohol became his escape. Leila eventually left. A year later, she filed for divorce.

Ricardo spiraled, drinking even more—until two years ago, when Lamberto rushed him to the ER. He was diagnosed with

Cirrhosis and has been undergoing treatment ever since, under strict orders to avoid alcohol.

When Ricardo looked up, Maria leaned forward slightly. "Sometimes, we revisit the past not just to relive the pain, but to remind ourselves that we survived it—and that there's no need to dwell there anymore. Once we understand this, we can forgive and let go. Do you agree?"

Ricardo met her gaze and nodded firmly.

"There are different kinds of pain," she continued softly. "Some fade. Others keep returning. Your love for Leila—and the memories—might bring pain back at times. Whether you see her or not, the longing may resurface until you fully move on or fall in love again. That's normal. Do you think this could be true?"

He bowed his head, trembling as he grappled with her words, caught between defiance and surrender. Maria saw it clearly: this was the delicate, shattering moment for her client-friend, where the raw truth struck deep, demanding to be confronted courageously.

"So," Maria asked gently, "when that pain returns… what could you do instead of drowning it in another bottle of vodka?"

A heavy silence settled. But Maria did not waver. She held her ground and waited patiently for his response. Her patience, a quiet, unyielding force, allowing ample time for her client-friend to face the truth and take the pivotal step himself.

Finally, Ricardo reached into his coat pocket and pulled out a folded paper—his "Action Plan."

He had created it during his first sessions with Maria after his diagnosis. It listed simple steps to take whenever sorrow or betrayal overwhelmed him. He once called it his "list of hope."

Maria's face softened. He had kept it all this time.

"Read it again," she urged.

Ricardo scanned the list quietly. "Yes… this still makes sense."

"Do you still believe in this plan?" she asked.

"Yes, Maria," he replied, looking her in the eye as he raised his mug in a small toast. The direct eye contact reassured her—his commitment was still alive.

"Do you believe these can truly help you?"

"Of course. They've been my go-to… until last night. I'm sorry," he whispered.

"Shush. That's why this list exists—to remind you there are many ways forward. And you can do them," Maria said firmly.

"Of course," Ricardo agreed with a faint smile.

"Will you follow them? And why?"

"Because they're the best solutions I have. And I know I can do them."

"You're brave, amigo," Maria said, smiling. "Looks like you won't be needing me much for now, huh? Just remember—you've done this before. You've already paved the right path. Just follow it."

"Thanks, Maria. It's always good to talk with you." Ricardo stood as Maria gathered her purse.

"Enjoy your coffee. I'll see you again here soon," she said warmly. "Café de Amor, my friend."

As she turned to leave, Lamberto hurried over, pulling out her chair.

"Your ride is here, Maria. On time as always. Thank you for coming by. We'll see you tomorrow?"

Maria smiled, and for a fleeting moment, Lamberto's heart skipped. Then he sat with Ricardo, ready to keep him company

.

* * *

Maria and The Stories She Keeps

"Tell Me My Story

Remembering may bring a gamut of emotions.

Sometimes, I may want to avoid the pain.

But again, without the pain,

How would I know the pleasures my life has brought?

Because the saddest part is when I cannot even remember any at all—

Like waking up always with a blank white sheet…

Nothing! And that is more painful to live with, day by day."

She wrote those words again in her gold-spiraled notebook. It was a personally crafted gift from Sofia, her caregiver. Maria loved those phrases. They were like her morning prayer. She would change the words now and then, but her message always stayed the same.

"How has your morning been, Madame Maria?" Zachary asked, flashing a charming smile as he watched her through the front mirror. "Ooooh, love your scarf. Goes well with your coat today. Don't you just wear nice clothes, Madame? Always chic! Every day—no fail!"

Maria shot a glance at this young man through the mirror and couldn't help but grin back.

"And so you are such a tease, Zachary! I am very well today. And how is your class going, huh? Are you behaving, young man?"

"Oh yes, Madame! I am always on top of the class. One more semester and I will be the main man for all these never-ending constructions," he said, nodding toward the ongoing roadworks as he drove his navy-blue sedan.

Zachary had mentioned to Maria that he was taking up a degree in Project Management at the University of Washington and would be graduating soon. He had signed up for Uber so he could support his studies.

He was such a fine young man—tall, dark, with just the right muscular physique. Yet his light-brown wavy hair softened his features, and his hazel eyes lit up whenever he talked. "I see through him so much. He is a good-looking boy,"

Maria often told herself, and she had grown fond of him from the first time he took her Uber request.

According to Zachary, he normally took Uber requests only in the afternoons, after his classes. But because Café de Amor was along his route to the university, he decided to take her request that first morning—and continued doing so for the second, third, and so forth.

At first, Maria found it odd that he constantly appeared for her rides, but eventually she agreed to his suggestion: he would be her regular "Good morning Uber driver" outside the app, under a private arrangement between them.

Once, she told Lamberto Amore that she was starting to like Zachary so much.

"He is very expressive and seems a hard-working boy—not to mention the good looks. He will certainly do well in his chosen career someday. I feel that by allowing him to pick me up every morning from your café, I am, somehow, able to help him. He is so jolly and optimistic, yet I sense he needs some help."

Lamberto nodded. "I think he misses his mom."

"You think so?" Maria wondered.

"Yes, I actually believe so, Maria," Lamberto declared wholeheartedly.

Maria wanted to pry more into Zachary's life, but she knew it wasn't the right time.

"Probably, one of these days, I will invite this cute boy for coffee," she secretly told herself. "I'd like to know him more. His personality is very interesting—actually, endearing!" Her thoughts made her smile broadly.

"I see that lovely smile, Madame," Zachary teased again. "But off you go. Have a fine day. I will pick you up tomorrow, alright?"

"Drive safely, young man. I love to see you soon," Maria said, feeling a curious giddiness in her heart.

"Oh no, I cannot fall for a younger guy," she laughed at her own thoughts as she stepped out of the car.

* * *

Immediately, Maria rushed through the massive halls of the Suzzallo Library, where she had been a contracted Library Associate for the past two years. The library is nestled at the heart of the University of Washington campus. It is one of the most-visited public libraries in the Seattle area, celebrated for its close resemblance to the fictional "Hogwarts Library" from the Harry Potter films.

Its gothic architecture evokes a sense of history and grandeur dating back to the 1920s. Tourists are always in awe of its iconic Reading Room, with its 65-foot-high vaulted ceilings and grand stained-glass windows. Its brass-lamped oak study tables and bookcases, bathed in colorful reflected light, create a truly magical atmosphere for learning.

Three years ago, after her release from the Pitié-Salpêtrière Hospital in Paris and her return to Seattle, Maria's first instinct to get her life back on track was to apply to libraries.

Having been in a deep coma for a year due to a tragic accident in France, she knew she could only rebuild her work habits in a place that offered both peace and quiet. A place where she could regain her skills while also having moments of discovery—or more aptly, "life recollection." A place where she could dig deep into herself, uncover what lay buried in the recesses of her core, and build a new foundation.

"I missed life in a slumber I did not choose. But I need to continue… so I can recall what I actually missed," she reminded herself every day as she pulled herself up to start afresh—again and again.

✳ ✳ ✳

Maria went straight to one of the back rooms she was assigned to for the day.

"Oh, how I love the smell of books," she often admitted.

She enjoyed rummaging through the books she sorted and organized, loved perusing their pages, and "re-learning" life from their stories. She soaked up authors' insights like a sponge. Her golden notebook had filled up with quotes, research notes, and fresh ideas that served as her daily dose of inspiration.

Yet more than what she gained from books, Maria cherished her interactions with colleagues and regular patrons. Most were students doing research; seniors catching up on their favorite authors' latest novels; immigrants trying to figure out "where and how to start life" in Seattle; or simply someone seeking "free public service."

All of them defined her daily significance. And in every conversation, she filled her "empty memory" with glimpses of their life stories.

"I may wake up blank every day. I am clueless about how I came about and what made me who I am. But I am also filled up with people's stories every day, Lamberto," she had shared in a few chats with him.

"They fill me up… for now. That is why I treasure my work at the Suzzallo. And going to your café. Talking to your clients is an honor."

Then she chuckled softly. "I am not a certified coach, right? You know that. However, I have the instinct to do this, Lamberto. Please believe me. I just know how to carry a conversation and help people light up," she declared, her eyes sparkling with pride and excitement.

"Even if it is for free, that is just okay. They don't know how important they make me feel. That is more than enough for me, Lamberto. Probably this is my career in my 'forgotten life,'" she laughed hard.

Lamberto simply smiled in agreement.

* * *

As Maria pushed her cart filled with new books down the aisle to the North Wing shelves, she took time to greet some of the regular patrons.

"Oh, hi, Mr. Smith. How are you finding that novel?" she asked.

"Halfway in it, Maria. The sun is out, so today is the perfect time to escape the house, get a hot drink, and read this book, huh?" Mr. Smith replied.

"Of course. Enjoy the day, Mr. Smith. I'll see you around," Maria said with a smile.

Then, whispering gently, "Hey, Alyssa. How is your job hunting?"

"Maria! So glad to see you. I have a scheduled job interview two days from now—just doing some research on the company. Wish me luck," Alyssa shared, touching Maria's arm. "I appreciate all the inputs you've given me. Thank you for helping me with the application and getting back my confidence. You enlightened me a lot."

As Maria moved on, she passed by teenagers with several books sprawled across their table. Their gentle whispers and lightly brushing hands didn't escape her attention.

"Library romance," Maria thought, and it gave her a young feeling as well.

"I wonder if I ever fell in love, too, in my past? Could there have been a special someone for me? Where is he now?" she mused.

"Well, anyway, if I ever did fall in love, I'm sure it would not have been in a library," she teased herself secretly.

* * *

A certain Greg Morgan approached her and asked if she was the "Coffee Coach" of Café de Amor. He said a friend had referred her as a good resource for help on a community project he was working on.

Maria laughed at the remark. "Oh, I do go there, Greg. I'm flattered, but I do not regard myself as one. However, we can talk and have coffee there this week."

They chatted a little more and agreed to take their discussion to Café de Amor the next time.

From afar, Nicholas was observing Maria. He looked up the moment he saw her walk through the hall. He didn't miss details of her appearance either.

"She's wearing her signature purple coat and scarf again. But I like her brown slacks today. Professional-looking, but very sweet, too," he said to himself.

Then Maria caught sight of him and waved happily. Nicholas waved back, feeling a bit shy.

* * *

Nicholas... The Wanderer

"Oh goodness! What is it with this balance sheet? I can't seem to reconcile it," Nicholas muttered, frustration evident in his voice. He reached for his cellphone and texted Matthew, his Chief Financial Officer (CFO): "Hey, boss, I need more time. Still working on this report. I'm well aware of our deadline, and I'll make sure it's on your desk before the day ends." He nervously tapped his fingers on his mahogany-colored electric standing desk and let out a relieved "Yohooo!" as he read Matthew's positive reply. Nicholas' office was on the 8th floor of one of the newest developments along Elliott Bay, part of the Puget Sound region, offering a majestic view of the Pacific Ocean in Seattle.

Nicholas was a stable, well-paid Certified Public Accountant (CPA) at one of Washington's prestigious accounting firms. He was nearing his 10th-year service anniversary with the company and was a top contender for the recently vacated Chief Accountant position. Detail-oriented, highly analytical, and with strong problem-solving skills, he was a stellar performer. Matching all his exceptional skills, as a professional, was his often business-like and stunning appearance. A head-turner, yet he exuded warmth and friendliness in his demeanor. Colleagues often said, "He has it all," and he seemed destined for the top of the career ladder. However, what set him apart, as his peers described, was his "gift of gab." His previous supervisor called his interpersonal and communication skills "amusingly unusual" for their field—a trait only Nicholas fully understood… until he met Maria.

Accountancy was never Nicholas' first choice. It was a path chosen by his parents. Though born and raised in Seattle, Nicholas was of Croatian descent. His family had migrated to Seattle, where they built a successful chain of European-inspired boutique and grocery stores, becoming one of the most prominent family businesses in downtown Seattle. Coming from an entrepreneurial lineage, his parents naturally expected Nicholas to pursue a career that would prepare him to run the family business someday. He had been dutiful so far.

But poetry and creative writing were Nicholas' true passions. He had suppressed this calling until his teenage years.

Ideas, words, and stories haunted him—tormenting him at night, in the shower, on the freeway, at school, or even among friends. At one point, he feared he was losing his sanity. He saw moments in "slow motion" and dreamt vivid, soap-opera-like plots. Anxious about his mental health, he secretly researched human psychology, reading books and watching documentaries, suspecting he might be experiencing depressive episodes or personality disorders. He never told anyone, not even his parents, fearing he would disappoint them or be ostracized in the world shaped for him. At 16, he created a highly encrypted blog called "The Secrets I Keep," where his creative side came alive. He confronted the "writer" within him and found "hope," which became his daily motivation. After college, he had written a vast collection of poems and stories that could have inspired and thrilled anyone's imagination—if he had shared them.

Unfortunately, Nicholas' blog remained a secret. His "wealth of literature" was for his eyes only. He lacked the confidence to share his gift with the world, unable to embrace a purpose other than the one his parents and society expected. "I am a corporate man, a businessman, and I have a family legacy to uphold. I cannot go astray," he often reminded himself.

That all changed the day he met Maria.

"Maria, my Coach," Nicholas sighed with satisfaction whenever he thought of her. "She gives me hope… courage," he told himself.

The first time Nicholas saw Maria enter Café de Amor, "time stood still." Like a scene from a movie, he swore he felt a gust of wind tousle his hair and gently lift strands of Maria's. He noticed every detail of her appearance: a dark purple coat, a light lavender scarf with a hood. As she entered the café, she pulled back her hood, revealing slightly grayed but copper-blond hair. She smiled, and Nicholas, mesmerized, wondered, "Does she know me? Why such a smile?" But Maria walked past him. As he followed her with his gaze, he saw her fingers brush against Lamberto's as she took her coffee from the café owner. Nicholas' heart skipped a beat. "Do I regret that she didn't notice me? Who is this woman?" he mused.

Nicholas approached Jasmin, the pink-haired barista who, unbeknownst to him, harbored a crush on him. "Hey, Jasmin, if you don't mind my asking, who's that lady with Lamberto?" he asked.

Jasmin glanced over and replied, "Oh, that's Maria. She's super popular here. She's our Coach Café—or, uh, Café Coach, I think? Maybe Coffee Coach?" She chuckled modestly. "Lamberto has a lot of troubled friends, you know," she teased, laughing. "Seriously, though, any regular who wants a deep conversation can talk to her," she added, winking at Nicholas. To Jasmin, it wasn't entirely a joke—she secretly hoped he'd turn his attention to her.

Nicholas missed the hint and pressed on. "What do you mean, 'talk to her'? Why do regulars talk to her?"

"The truth? She's amazing. She listens well—like the mother you'd want to open up to when the world sucks," Jasmin said, rolling her eyes playfully. "Kidding aside, I wouldn't be here without Lamberto and Maria. Lamberto gave me a job when I was lining up at a shelter. He asked if I had a full-time job to keep my housing. I told him that was my problem—I couldn't keep a job! I'd been evicted from one shelter to another." Jasmin paused, reflecting on her past. She had grown up in foster homes until adulthood. "I took the job here, and Lamberto introduced me to Maria. And look, I'm still here, keeping a job!" Nicholas felt a pang of empathy as Jasmin continued, "I cried buckets, but Maria stayed. She listened and even paid for my coffee," she laughed. "Then, a few sessions later, she threw me off. She started asking hard questions— ones that hurt." She paused again.

Nicholas waited, intrigued. In a soft whisper, Jasmin continued, "…Yet those questions, tough as they were, were things I wanted to answer. And when I started working through them with Maria, things began to fall into place—

slowly but surely." She looked into Nicholas' eyes, and he held her gaze, sensing a bond forming. Yet, he also felt a growing excitement to learn more about Maria.

"You said any regular can talk to her? Do you…" he trailed off.

Surprised but supportive, Jasmin jumped in. "Oh, you want to talk to her, Nicky? Give it a try?"

"Uh…" Nicholas hesitated, second-guessing himself but feeling compelled. "Yeah, I guess. Do I need an appointment?"

Jasmin, curious but hiding it, asked, "You okay, Nicky? You sure about this?" She seemed worried for him.

"I'm good, Jasmin! Don't worry, okay? It's nothing serious," he said, patting her arm with a smile. "Just a task I want to start… and finish, I guess. She might help. You recommend her, right?" He winked. Jasmin, caught off-guard by the warmth of the interaction, beamed. "Of course, well-recommended," she said, flashing her cutest smile. "Just be here early before someone takes that spot," she added, pointing to the chair across from Maria, where Lamberto sat.

"Okay, I'll be here tomorrow," Nicholas promised as he headed for the door.

Jasmin called after him, "And, Nicky, if she's not available, I'm here!" Nicholas turned, gave a thumbs-up, and walked on. Secretly, Jasmin wished he'd seek her out instead.

Nicholas' sessions with Maria spanned six fruitful conversations over four months, scheduled at various intervals based on his needs.

During their final talk, Nicholas began secretly following Maria. "What a romantic stalker I've become," he teased himself. In the mornings, he exchanged pleasantries with her at Café de Amor. He noticed she had "chats or talks" with other regulars too. During lunch breaks, he drove to the Suzzallo Library just to catch a glimpse of her, often hiding to observe from afar. On early days off, he even followed her home, learning she lived with her caregiver, Sofia.

At night, he wrote about her—recalling their talks, her advice, her insights, and bits of information he gathered from Lamberto and the café crew. "No, I can't be obsessed with this mysterious lady. But somehow, she needs me as much as I need her. I want to be courageous for her," he told himself. Despite his growing fascination, his sleep had never been more peaceful. He felt a satisfaction he'd never known before.

"Okay, this report's done!" he exclaimed, texting Matthew. "On my way to the boardroom, boss!" Glancing at his watch, he murmured, "Gee, past 2 p.m. Gotta grab a late lunch after." He dropped off the report, rode the glass elevator, and marveled at the ocean view below. He stepped into the employee parking lot, slid into his white Tesla Model X SUV, and thought, "What a toxic day. A good coffee, a BLT, and a trip to Suzzallo—that'll make my day."

Nicholas knew he had almost everything: a promising career, a supportive social circle, and a family fortune laid out for him. Yet, deep in his heart, there was a void he'd been trying to fill. For the first time, he was embarking on something that sparked true delight in his soul. And he knew Maria was a big part of it.

Nicholas was beginning to embrace the greatest calling of his life.

* * *

Cheers to All the Tête-à-Tête

"Tête-à-tête… what an interesting word," Nicholas remarked.

"It's French for a private conversation between two people—an exchange, a chat, a meeting of minds," Maria explained, raising her coffee mug in a cheerful toast.

"I see…" Nicholas mused, pondering the term.

"Just relax, Nicky! Is it okay if I call you Nicky?" Maria asked. Nicholas nodded. "This isn't formal. It's just me getting to know you and you getting to know me. In our chats, building trust is key. We must be genuine with each other, and we'll build that trust together." Her eyes twinkled as she smiled.

"That smile is certainly captivating," Nicholas thought, listening intently.

"Let's be open with one another and create a safe space where you can share what matters to you," Maria continued. "I'll start. My full name is Maria Lemaire," she said, emphasizing her last name with a playful hand gesture. "I was born here, but my parents are French. Most of my relatives, so I'm told, live in Paris. I've never met any of them, except for a close cousin, Emily, who still lives there. So, if you're expecting sweet French phrases from me, I'm afraid I'll disappoint you." She flashed another warm smile.

"I can't spill my whole life story yet," she added with a chuckle. "I'm still piecing the puzzle together myself." Nicholas thought she was joking, missing the sincerity in her words. "But I've spent my life here in Seattle. I work at Suzzallo Library—you should visit sometime if you haven't in a while," she teased. "I always tell new friends I meet here at Café de Amor to check it out. Not just because I work there— I truly love it. There's something calming about being surrounded by books. Do you love reading, Nicholas?"

Nicholas wanted to exclaim, "Yes, I do!" but restrained the excitement creeping up his spine. His curiosity about where this conversation might lead was growing. "I used to," he replied cautiously, "but I've been busy with work lately."

"Tell me more about yourself, Nicholas. What interests you?" Maria asked.

"I'm a math person, as they say. I ended up in the corporate world. I've been good at it, but…" He paused, wondering if he should steer the conversation toward his true purpose for meeting.

Maria sensed the shift instantly. Her keen instinct, honed as a coach, picked up the urgency in his hesitation. She knew this was the moment. "But something's bothering you, isn't it, Nicky? What do you want to talk about? Are you ready to share?"

With that simple question, Maria widened the "safe space" between them. Over their sessions, Nicholas gradually lowered his guard as trust in Maria grew.

Maria soon discovered the "artist" trapped within Nicholas—the spark that fueled his passion and joy. As a coach, she understood that her observations were not hers to impose. Her role was to guide clients to uncover truths themselves. "I'm only a catalyst for change," she reminded herself, resisting the urge to reveal too much. Patience was her virtue, and the coaching process, which she viewed as a friendship, had to be owned by her clients. "This is always about them," she affirmed.

With Nicholas, Maria aimed to help him embrace that "becoming a writer" was vital to who he was—not a threat to his established life but a piece that could complete his purpose.

He could be both a business and creative man, fulfilling his and his parents' goals. By committing to both, he could merge his skills into one great calling, creating a richer life for himself and inspiring others.

The "how" and "when" were challenges Maria would guide Nicholas through. Their tête-à-têtes led to profound discoveries for both.

* * *

Nicholas' AHA! Moments

Through many candid conversations, Nicholas confronted truths that propelled his transformation. Maria called these his "breakthrough moments"—when burdens lifted, blindfolds fell, and what was once unclear became crystal clear. These "AHA moments" required honesty, humility, and openness, cultivated through courageous talks over several meetups.

* * *

Maria: "Why do you hide your talent for creative writing, Nicky? What are you afraid of?"

Nicholas: "It's not lucrative, right? It feels good, but it won't put food on the table, as they say. It's not the career people think suits me or secures my future family. If I get too caught up, I might lose my job or the family business…"

Maria: "Why would you lose your job or fail the family business if you pursue writing? Can't you write on the side while honoring your family's legacy? Can't you craft one story at a time in your free moments?"

Through Maria's challenging questions, Nicholas unraveled the baseless assumptions he'd held about being a writer. His fears—about what his parents or others might say—were clichés he'd fabricated. He realized he had no evidence anyone would reject his gift, especially since they hadn't seen it. He'd created his own fear and self-doubt. Ultimately, Nicholas saw it didn't have to be one or the other. With proper time management, he could nurture all his gifts. "Writing is one of them," he acknowledged, starting small as a hobby. "No one and nothing will be at risk, and I'll be happier." For the first time, he made peace with this truth.

* * *

Nicholas: "Maria! I finally made my blog, The Secrets I Keep, public. You won't believe it, but I've gained over a hundred followers in weeks, and the numbers are growing! I haven't even written new posts—just my existing collection is getting positive feedback. I have readers who appreciate my thoughts!"

Maria: "Why doubt yourself, Nicky? Now that you've taken this step, what will keep your passion alive?"

Nicholas: "Keep believing in myself?"

Maria: "That's inspiring, Nicky. What else will help you believe in yourself?"

Nicholas: "My purpose—the reason I'm doing this."

Maria: "Why, Nicky? What's your purpose?"

Nicholas: "When I write, I share another side of myself. I speak truths others relate to. I feel my soul, I feel them, and I feel more human. They get inspired, too. Writing may not always be my livelihood, but it's my ultimate dream, my most passionate calling. Doing it alongside my corporate life lets me inspire others while keeping the spark of living alive in me."

Maria smiled. She knew she must continue helping Nicholas reinforce his purpose. Writing, like life, has ups and downs. One can get lost in its bliss or derailed by setbacks. Necessary pauses to recalibrate goals or reroute paths are part of growth. But a clear purpose, like a beacon, keeps one steering forward, even through pain. In time, that purpose deepens into a lifelong commitment.

* * *

Maria: "What's holding you back now, Nicky? How's work? Your family? Is writing affecting them?"

Nicholas: "No, Maria. You were right. My family and colleagues cheer me on with my blog. They respect this side of me, and I have their full support. It's not affecting my career either—I just got promoted! But why do I feel stuck? My creative juices aren't flowing. Nothing's coming out. Why do I feel I'm not growing, just repeating myself?"

Maria: "Let's think this through. If writing is a way of life to enjoy, how do you enrich yourself? How do you sustain happiness in it?"

This conversation sparked a commitment. Nicholas realized passion, like any essential in life, must be nurtured. He began researching, reading biographies of favorite novelists, and gathering tips from their struggles and successes. Within a month, he joined writing workshops and conferences, meeting like-minded writers and exploring new techniques. His corporate stature connected him with publishing industry leaders, igniting an interest in writing a book. Unbeknownst to him, this pursuit would uncover another gift—one that would unexpectedly repay Maria, his friend, confidante, and coach.

* * *

Nicholas: "I can't start, Maria! I'm stuck! It's been a month, and my mind is blank—no subject for my novel!"

Maria: "A writer needs inspiration, Nicky. It may not be in your head yet, so look into your heart. What's in that big heart of yours? Who inspires you? Listen closely, and when you find your muse, follow it. That muse will lead you to a story that inspires the world."

That final tête-à-tête sparked Nicholas' months-long "stalking" of Maria. Unbeknownst to her, she had revealed his ultimate muse—herself. The world is full of twists and turns that connect every living soul in it. Maria cleared the cobwebs in Nicholas' mind, freeing the writer within. Yet, unknown to him, the power of his words would answer Maria's prayers. By mustering the courage to write a book about her, Nicholas wielded a power that would whisk away the dark clouds obscuring her memory lane.

* * *

Jasmin… When Love Strikes Hard

"What's eating you up, Jasmin?" Roy, one of Lamberto's long-time and trusted baristas, asked. "What's between you and Nicholas there? You smiled at him when you gave his coffee like a love-struck teenager. Then, now you are literally in tantrums. You are vexing us here, girl."

"Am I, Roy? That obvious? Really?" Jasmin queried, quite perturbed with her own actions.

"Oh yeah! But you are being like that to me and the rest of the crew only. Not with your lover boy there. You were all smiles to him just a while ago, huh? From an indelible smirk since you arrived to open the shop this morning; suddenly, your face totally lit up when you handed Nicholas his cup. Oh, pleasantries here and there, then, when your crush turned away—gee, you transformed back. That smirk is all over you again. You are a tough nut to crack today," Roy complained. "Come on! Spill the beans. Did he do something? Is he being unfair with you?"

"I am okay, Roy. Just confused. And yes, love-struck. He is such a catch. Never had a boyfriend before, you know. I love all the dating. He is the first guy who seriously brought me out lavishly. You know, when a guy takes you out to nice places— expensive or not, but real decent ones—you can't help but think you may be special to him too, right? Been almost three months now. But I am sensing he doesn't feel the same way," Jasmin confessed, heartbroken. "He cares but not the same way. Something is really off..." Her words trailed on. Suddenly, seemingly about to cry, she said, "Excuse me for a sec," and rushed to the crew's locker room.

Roy knew better than to follow her at that time. He fully understood she needed the moment to gather herself. And it was the morning peak hours for the café, too. The shop was certainly a full house at that time. Even the café's "mini-rooms," a special feature it offers, were all filled up with several ongoing "meet-ups." That included the room where Lamberto and Maria were having their chat. However, amidst going to the espresso machine to assembling beverages in queue, Roy managed to observe Nicholas more. He took note of Nicholas' regular chats with Maria and Lamberto these days.

"Well, this guy seems oblivious to Jasmin's feelings. Actually, he has never been so babbly until he made friends with Maria. Oh goodness, my girl Jasmin is on her way to a heartbreak. Though, I really hope I am wrong," he murmured to himself.

When Jasmin came back, "You feeling better, Jasmin?" Roy implored.

"You're a sweet, Roy. I think I am. I will be okay. Sorry to worry you. By the way, I am meeting him again tonight. In Fogo de Chao." She forced a smile.

Roy blew a whistle. "Wow, fancy! That guy is really something," impressed by Jasmin's disclosure. Fogo de Chao is among the posh restaurants in the Seattle area, famous for its Brazilian steak and long list of vintage wine.

"I know, right? And so you may ask what is this all about?" She looked straight into Roy's eyes and whispered, "I told you. Dating him is always a special time for me. He is generous and lavish. But, Roy, all these are fabulous until he began asking more and more about Maria." She bowed her head and pretended to be occupied with washing the mugs. "It was all romantic in the first few dates. Then, slowly, I noticed we were already discussing her. Not us. But about her! Maria? I was lured into sharing whatever I know." She looked up to Roy, and he saw distress in her eyes. "Then, he even asked about Ricardo, Lamberto, Zachary… Sofia?" Jasmin elaborated.

This caught Roy by surprise. "Sofia…? How come… how did…?" Roy was dumbfounded.

"Yes, Roy." She hesitated for a moment, then, "You heard me right. The scariest thing is he knows about Sofia. He confessed that he had been following Maria around. He knows where she works, lives…" Jasmin paused a bit, then opened up what disturbed her most. "That's why he learned about Sofia, too. I know he is up to something, Roy. I am worried as well for Maria. Why will he do that? I am truly baffled. I cannot explain. Yet, despite it all, I also don't want to stay away." And when she held Roy's stunned look, Roy swore she was at the verge of crying again.

Trying to gather his composure, Roy advised, "If you have a strong gut feel he is just using you, have you confessed this to Lamberto? Have you cautioned him… for everyone's safety?"

Jasmin nodded that she did. "And? What did Lamberto say?" Roy prodded more.

"Not to worry about it, for now. That is what he said," Jasmin shared, but she was lost more in her thoughts.

Then with a hint of panic, Roy asked, eyes wide with anxiety, "Hey, Jasmin! Did you tell him everything? All we know about Maria?"

Jasmin ran back to the locker room and silently wept for all her fears, confusion, and repressed love. She was torn apart by her friendship with Maria, loyalty to Lamberto, and fondness for one who could probably be her first ever true love—no matter how shady Nicholas seemed to be. For someone who did not grow up with her own real family, who never stayed long in one place to make real friends, choosing one over the other would be the hardest. Everyone and all she came across with at Café de Amor had become her "core circle" for quite some time now. "The family I never had"— the truth she acknowledged for her own peace. And so, as such, Jasmin was left no choice but to wish and pray that she would not have to break it at all.

* * *

Lamberto's Leap of Faith

"Do you miss working overseas, Lamberto?" Ricardo asked.

"I do. But no regrets, amigo," Lamberto honestly assured Ricardo. "As they say, retiring can do one good if taken at the right time. I guess circumstances have forced me to appreciate that now," he said with a heavy sigh. "Time is a gift. Now, I have that in my control. It is just that, sometimes, I admit, it is hard to make ends meet," he laughed a little, throwing up his arms in the air as a gesture of resignation to his current state, while pointing at the entire inside of Café de Amor. "That is why I snatch whatever odd jobs are out there, my friend. Your old man here can still take on much."

When Lamberto de Amore retired from his professional career more than four years ago, he opened up a coffee shop and named it after himself—Café de Amor. Incidentally, because he was born and raised in Madrid, Spain, and his family name Amore technically means "love," he envisioned a business that would promote "nothing less than the advocacy of giving back." However, since his professional background had always been in the field of engineering and government service, establishing Café de Amor was a tall order that he had to accomplish from scratch. With the help of friends like Ricardo and Roy, who had connections and expertise in the coffee business, Lamberto learned the ropes quite well. With such a loyal Café Crew, he succeeded in shaping and popularizing the concept of Café de Amor. To set it apart from the many throbbing coffee shops in Seattle, his team marketed Café de Amor not just as a "coffee shop," but as a "talk shop" or a "social hub"—a place where people could converge. It is an interesting-looking coffee shop from the outside, but with dynamic "other rooms" inside… "Where the real magical aroma is felt," as noted in one of the testimonies of a regular customer.

Right at the center of the shop is an exquisite French-inspired interior. One is first allured by an enormous glassed counter that appealingly displays different kinds of pastries and sandwiches—from European croissants, éclairs, and muffins, to Spanish empanadas and all sorts of American ready-to-go breakfast sandwiches. The simplicity yet clarity of how they are displayed in one grand showcase effectively creates instant gastronomic excitement, one that is hard to resist. As one customer testified: "I was in a hurry just to grab any coffee the first time. But I could not forget all these pastries that, the next day, I had to come back. Lamberto has a sure way of teasing us back on!"

At the end of such a luscious display is the elegant Le Comptoir—the counter table, designed with a mix of vintage and modern materials to give it a stunning look. Standing by it is the "Barista of the Hour," with apron "spick and span," ready to begin the first customer interaction with a greeting: "Good day, Sir / Madame! Your wake-up coffee starts now. What could it be?" Behind the counter are the heavy-duty espresso machines, coffee grinders, and brewing equipment where Café de Amor's other friendly baristas work their magic.

The shop offers a wide variety of coffee drinks brewed exclusively from the finest beans produced in Washington State. Lamberto ensured that he maintained strong connections with the native farmers and local producers of the state. He wanted Café de Amor to be popularly known as "the unique French bistro that promotes the Seattle aroma." In one of his local TV interviews, he was heard saying:

"I envision Café de Amor to be your morning inspiration, whatever fickle weather you find yourself in. As they say, the sun in Seattle comes out only about 46% of the year. Our sun here is shy, hidden behind clouds most of the time. It drizzles or rains for 155 days—but honestly, I think even more! Yet we cannot deny that we wake up to the best morning mist. Such fresh air mixed with the smell of pines. Evergreen State, indeed! We also get great snows in winter. But what makes it so unique here is that, sometimes, we get to experience all four seasons in a single day! It shines now; it rains in a minute; it hails or snows right after. It changes every minute! You never know what to bring outside. Depending on how we see it, we, Washingtonians, always face the adaptability challenge of an ever-changing climate. And it is that fickleness that makes us ready for excitement all day long. That is the joy of living here—in Seattle! So when we brew and send you off with that aroma, we want you to be excited to start your day. Get up proud and say… Ahh! That's my Seattle!"

Lamberto received raving reviews from that interview, which went viral. It contributed to the growing influx of Café de Amor's regulars.

Yet that inviting aroma does not remain confined to the center of the bistro where regulars enjoy their beverages. It spreads outward to the next "unique deal" the shop offers: the mini-business rooms that surround the French bistro. Regulars can reserve these rooms for an hourly fee to host meetings, group studies, and workshops. Unlike the center interior, which is intricately dramatic and elegant, the rooms are deliberately straightforward and business-like in appearance. Thus, as a whole, Café de Amor exudes an eclectic ambiance that suits diverse needs. These "meet-up rooms" are additional attractions that entice Café de Amor's regulars to stay and keep coming back.

"We want you to enjoy the best coffee and food you will find in Seattle. But we also want to go beyond that. We want Café de Amor to serve as an opportunity for the community to interact and engage more. We want to be part of your social lives. We want to provide a space for your work, your creative time, or simply your personal moment. We want to be your constant companion," Lamberto explained further in his interview.

In one of these "meet-up rooms," Maria often stayed to chat with customers and enjoy her coffee. There, she added her personal touch of magic to the shop and its loyal patrons. As reported in The Seattle Times and aired on King 5 Channel:

"Café de Amor offers a bizarre yet stimulating concept in the coffee business. Maria Lemaire is gaining popularity as the 'Ms. Congeniality' of the shop. Folks are coming in to check her out, and so far, they all leave with satisfied cups of coffee— along with stories of how their mindsets were transformed positively. Ms. Lemaire vehemently declined any interviews, for now, but the Café crew wants us to put on record that she is not a professional coach. They say she is just a regular at Café de Amor and a friend for a hearty chat…"

For Lamberto, however, venturing into Café de Amor was a lifetime risk. "It was a leap of faith," he confessed. It required him to leave his professional comfort zone, face his fears, start completely anew, and gamble his entire retirement and life savings to finance the business. "I am only guided by love… and faith," he shared in his interviews.

Lamberto de Amore is a first-generation U.S. immigrant. Backed by his excellent academic record, he was granted a full engineering scholarship at Seattle University. Since his college days, he had fallen deeply in love with the city. Thus, after graduation, he applied for U.S. naturalization, started his career, and eventually raised a family.

In his early thirties, Lamberto's biggest professional break came when he landed a contractual job at the U.S. Embassy in Manila, Philippines. His performance earned him a reputable name. Building on that experience, he soon established his own company, Amore Consulting Engineers, which provided a wide range of engineering and maintenance services. The company became a regular contractor of the U.S. government. With such accountability, Lamberto managed projects in various U.S. military bases outside the country. For twenty-five years, he lived and traveled across Europe, Asia, and U.S. territories. Wherever there was a U.S. military base, chances were that Lamberto had worked there. As his wife always described him, he had become a "man of the world."

His contracts varied from one to five years in a single location, with only short vacations back to Seattle to see his wife and children. At times, he relocated his family to the Philippines, the United Kingdom, Italy, and Guam. Those were cherished times, as they shared and learned different cultures together. All the perks they enjoyed as a family were "personal gifts" that he took pride in. He believed he had given them privileges that not all fathers could provide.

Unfortunately, his family never stayed longer than six months with him in one place. Painful as it was, Lamberto knew that his wife and children would have more stable lives if they resided permanently in the United States. Though he ensured his presence for significant family occasions and celebrations in Seattle, he missed the simple joys of fatherhood: driving them to school, playing outdoors, listening to their growing-up issues. His communication with them was always open and flowing, yet he knew there were countless days when his physical presence would have meant more.

"Sorry, my love. I have invested so much to realize this business dream. But being away from you and the children is the trade-off I must accept every day to sustain it. I am sorry I chose this path to support our family. I am sorry…" he confessed to his wife through phone calls and love letters during the endless lonely nights he endured on military bases.

"Do not worry, my love," his wife assured him. "Your children will grow up knowing the risks and sacrifices you bear for us and for our country. During moments when they ache for you, I will explain how lonelier you are without us. When they are fearful, I will make them understand how you remain faithful and courageous amidst the threats and struggles you face each day. I will ensure they see beyond what they miss from you, my love. Your children will admire you for your unconditional love. They will grow up responsible and selfless like their father. They will respect you, my dear, until our last breath," his wife echoed with love.

Lamberto was always grateful for the strong woman she had been through so many years of their marriage. Yet, like all unions, theirs was tested by fire. Given their circumstances, Lamberto's wife never had a steady career of her own. She dedicated all her time and energy to their children, the household, and overseeing Lamberto's central office in Seattle whenever needed. Her hands were always full with his and their children's needs.

When their children reached their teenage years, however, she went through a depression phase of mid-life. From the hardships of their long-distance love affair, her fortitude wavered. The once steady home became filled with worries and uncertainties.

"We have robbed you of your youth, my dear. You have given all you have for us, but we have neglected that you have dreams, too," Lamberto ruefully confessed. "Forgive me. Find your calling now—whatever it is that will lift the burdens in your heart. We will support you. I may not be there by your side, but the children are grown now. We will manage on our own. Please, follow your dreams," he lovingly offered.

Lamberto's wife had earned a degree in Child Psychology at Seattle University, the very campus where they met and fell in love. However, right after graduation, they married, and she never pursued a personal career. She thought she would forever be content supporting Lamberto's dreams for their family.

"But I was wrong, Lamberto. I should have loved myself, too. I lost myself in loving you. I don't know my worth anymore," she helplessly wailed to her husband.

During this "mid-life crisis," she came across coaching—a career possibility growing in popularity at the time in the field of human development. Lamberto and their children were ecstatic with her newfound passion. She immediately got certified, and for almost a year, she offered pro bono coaching services to establish her credibility. Yet, as the coaching industry grew competitive, her renewed hope dwindled. Unknown to Lamberto and their children, she had been diagnosed with symptoms of manic depression.

"Please, Lamberto. Please come home. I need you now," she begged him.

Realizing the seriousness of the call to save his marriage, Lamberto promised his wife that he would retire and permanently relocate back to Seattle with her by their 25th wedding anniversary.

"My greatest gift to you, dearest wife. You will never be alone again," he shared his decision.

Her condition—characterized by extreme mood swings between mania (highs) and depression (lows)—meant that Lamberto's news brought her completely to a state of elation. She began making plans for his ultimate homecoming.

"And what will you do, Lamberto, when you retire here?" she teased him during their long talks.

"We will sell the company and I will just be a stay-at-home husband, preparing your meals and coffee every day," he replied.

"Oh! That would be sweet! You will be my personal barista then, huh?" she chuckled.

"Ah, that gives me an idea, my love," Lamberto agreed.

"But dear, would you still allow me to do coaching? I still want to grow in this profession," his wife asked.

"Of course, my dear. I promise you my support all the way," Lamberto answered.

She kept that promise ardently in her heart.

However, on the second night of their anniversary trip in Aspen, with their children, Lamberto sadly broke the news that he was deferring his retirement for one more year. "I need more time to roll out the company sale," he explained. The children were heartbroken but they understood. Lamberto's wife, however, was devastated and enraged. Throughout the remaining days of their trip, she hardly slept. He noticed the signs of insomnia and weight loss. Shattered by his own decision, he began to question his integrity.

But it was too late. The morning after their return to Seattle, they awoke to a letter from Lamberto's wife:

"I have left to find myself…"

No one knew her plan or destination until the tragic news arrived that completely turned their world upside down.

On the many nights Lamberto waited for her, he wrote her love letters:

It has been years

And I still find it strange

I still cry over your loss

I still feel we have not had it all?

Though we travelled far and wide

Shared dreams for you and I

Laughed and cried and fought for us

Still, I am unsure if we had enough?

So I say my endless sorry every day

Forgive me, dear. Please come back!

My dreams of you shall never fade

I wish you will find your way home, at last!

Only faith keeps me waiting on

Faith… that, one day, you may look my way

Faith… that when you finally see me

You will know… "I stayed for you, my love!"

* * *

Sofia – A Daughter is a Daughter All Her Life

"1, 2, 3… Camera, roll… Action!" she shouted. Sofia stood up from her director's chair. The Arizona heat was blinding her eyes, and she adjusted her khaki snapback cap slightly to get a better view of the scene. Despite her cool, plain cotton shirt and loose, baggy khaki walking shorts, she was sweating profusely in the nearly 85°F temperature. Her copper-blonde hair was tied up in a bun, and without her sunglasses, her hazel eyes reflected a lighter tone in the sun's brightness. At first glance, no one would guess she was the headstrong leader of this production team. In her casual attire, she looked more like a teenager than the director of this suspenseful action-thriller.

They were shooting her favorite scene, and there was no way she would let it be anything less than perfect. She silently motioned to the cameraman on her left to change his angle. She signaled for a full view of the majestic Grand Canyon in slow motion. After a few shots, she directed another crew member to shift the camera toward the main lead. Ruggedly handsome Tom Hindman, riding a black stallion, sashayed confidently along the dry rim trail of the canyon. The horse's strong gallops kicked up huge clouds of dust behind him, emphasizing his entrance and the dramatic features of this hero.

"Sofia? Sofia? Are you there?" Annie's voice called out.

Sofia snapped awake from her dream. "Oh no, I fell asleep!" she mumbled hastily to herself. By instinct, she tidied her hair with her hands, exhaled to compose herself, and immediately turned on the camera on her laptop screen. "I'm here, Annie," she declared. "How long have you been there? Sorry! But yeah, I'm good now. What's up?" she said.

"Oh, just a few seconds, Sofia. No big deal. I'm confirming that I sent the requirements for the Singapore shipping before I get some rest. Can you let me know if you received them?" Annie, Sofia's team leader, asked.

Sofia checked her inbox. "Yup, all looks good, Annie. I'll review the documents thoroughly and, after due diligence, I'll ship them off," she replied confidently. Sofia worked as a virtual assistant for Annie Snider, Procurement Team Leader at an international logistics company. Annie was based in London, and Sofia's task was to review all shipping documents during Annie's off-hours, as proper review and document handling were time-sensitive aspects of the business. Sofia had adapted well to the virtual setup during her first few months, and Annie was impressed with her meticulous approach. Over time, Annie and Sofia had built a strong, long-distance work rapport that suited them both.

"I'll take care of this, Annie, and I'll keep you posted. Bye!" Sofia assured her as she ended the chat. "Gee, that was a close one," she laughed to herself, standing up to grab an energy drink from her fridge.

As she lounged back on her sofa, her phone rang. "Hi, Auntie Emily! How have you been?" Sofia greeted excitedly.

"Je vais bien," Emily responded in French, letting her niece know she was doing well. Emily Lemaire-Debuois was a licensed psychologist with her own clinic in Paris. She had earned her bachelor's degree in psychology at the University of Washington, where she learned about life in the United States and grew close to her cousin, Maria Lemaire, who had hosted her in Seattle during her studies. Later, Emily returned to France to marry her longtime partner, a medical degree holder, and together they opened their own clinic. They had been married for over twenty years and had two grown sons, Jason and Jules, who were the same age as Sofia. "Is cousin Maria there?" Emily asked.

"Not yet. She'll be home in an hour or two. But I'm glad you called," Sofia replied.

"Of course! I wanted to call as soon as I could, my dear Sofia. You make me one proud auntie. You're so awesome! Congratulations!" Emily's voice brimmed with excitement. "I heard you got another dream job offer. When do you plan to leave for California? Have you told Maria? And don't worry, dear, we can arrange for Maria's new companion," she said, eager to hear about Sofia's plans.

"Silence fell on Sofia's end. "Sofia? What's wrong, dear? You've always wanted this job, right? Filmmaking is your dream," Emily prompted.

"I do… I did. But, Auntie Emily, it's not the right time yet. I have faith something like this will come my way again," Sofia explained hesitantly. "I don't think I can leave… Mom," she added, pausing on the endearment.

"Sofia, let's think this through, my dear. You've sacrificed so much for three years already. This is the third dream job offer you've declined to stay with your mom. You don't have to keep doing this. Your father feels the same way," Emily said gently.

"Did he call you about this, Auntie? How many times have I explained to both of you that I'm doing well with my job now? I like my virtual assistant job. It pays well, and I don't have to deal with commuting or rushing to get ready for work every day. I'm fine with this setup. I can relax and get paid," Sofia clarified, half-joking.

"This isn't the job for you, my dear. You need to go out, meet people your age, date, mingle," Emily said cautiously.

"Let me stop you there, Auntie. These are modern times, and virtual jobs are the trend now. They're significant in today's fast-paced, tech-driven world. Come on! It even pays better than many of your so-called real jobs out there," Sofia argued politely. "Plus, I like the extra allowance I get from you and Dad for being Mom's caregiver," she added playfully. "Of course, I don't want to give that up!"

"But you love California. You're a top-notch graduate from UCLA with a degree in filmmaking that you haven't used yet. Last year, you got two incredible offers from Universal Studios and Lionsgate, and you turned them both down! Now it's Warner Brothers, Sofia. Please give this serious thought. There's nothing wrong with your job now, and we respect it, but we know this isn't what you set out to do. I'm sure your mom would want to see you use your talents fully," Emily said lovingly.

"Mom…" The name echoed in Sofia's mind. "She needs me now, more than ever. I have to look after her." She sighed heavily.

Sensing her niece was rapt again with senseless guilt, Emily broke the silence. "Three years ago, when we planned this, we agreed you'd pose as her caregiver temporarily, Sofia, just until we could arrange her relocation back to Seattle, where she belongs. Our goal was to let familiar people and places help her regain her sense of self. After two years, we're indebted to you for helping your mom establish her routines. Now, we wait for her recovery to take its natural course. As the doctors advised, she should progress at her own pace. We can hire a licensed caregiver now, someone trained to care for patients with post-traumatic amnesia, like your mom, my dearest cousin. But we owe it to Maria to live our lives fully as she journeys toward her awakening. Your mother never expected anything in return for the love she gave you. She'd be heartbroken if she recognized you now and learned you've thrown away promising opportunities for her. You have to fulfill her dreams for you, Sofia," Emily said, her voice cracking as she reflected on Maria's condition.

Sofia was Maria's eldest child. She was in her senior year at UCLA, pursuing a degree in Film, Television, and Digital Media, when Maria's tragic accident occurred in Melun, France. Maria had been on a night express train from Nice to

Paris, where she had spent nearly two months on what she called her "personal retreat," when it collided with a goods train at Melun station. Emily and her husband, David, were waiting for her at the Paris station, but she never arrived.

As Maria's only kin in France, Emily was the first to receive the tragic news that Maria was among the casualties and had been rushed to the Hospital Center de Melun. According to rescuers, Maria had helped secure injured children and elders to safety before collapsing from her own injuries and exhaustion.

Emily and David arranged for Maria's transfer to Pitié-Salpêtrière Hospital in Paris, where they had access to medical support. Then, Emily faced the difficult task of informing Maria's family in Seattle and apologizing for allowing Maria's retreat in France a secret to them. Maria's family flew to Paris immediately, but for months, she remained in a coma. Emily supported the family, just as Maria had supported her during her college years in Seattle.

When Maria awoke, she was diagnosed with retrograde amnesia, a condition that prevented her from recalling memories before the accident. Emily and her physicians introduced information about her past gradually. "No, I don't understand what you're saying. Why can't I remember anything?" Maria would wail in frustration. Sessions overwhelmed her, and she lost control. When her family was introduced, she became petrified at their silhouettes and fell into another coma for three months. "She was just not ready to see them yet," Emily contemplated. When Maria woke up, it was only Emily that she remembered from her past. Devastated, her family returned to Seattle.

Maria stayed with the Dubois family in Paris for several more months. Emily acted as her personal psychologist, attending to her needs. Based on her experience, Emily knew Maria's recovery might take time. "Her mind has a barrier protecting her from deep anguish," she explained to Maria's husband. "The accident was the final trigger to shield herself from the pain she was escaping from. It's like self-preservation. It's good that she remembers me, even if I am very much part of her past. We'll have to let her process at her own pace until she's ready to forgive and be strong again." The family found comfort in Maria's growing enjoyment of Paris life, and Emily encouraged them to prepare for her eventual return to Seattle.

Sofia used the waiting period to complete her degree, graduating top of her class but choosing not to attend the ceremony without her mother. When she learned of Emily and her father's plan to help Maria ease back into Seattle life, she pleaded to be a part of it.

Maria's husband purchased a luxurious flat in one of Seattle's newest residential buildings. He gave Sofia free reign to furnish it, knowing if there is anyone who took after Maria's taste in homemaking, it would be her, their only daughter. Maria had raised Sofia well, and they had always called themselves "the best of friends." After the tragedy, Sofia harbored resentment toward her father and avoided him at all cost. However, their shared efforts to prepare for Maria's return to Seattle brought them closer again, and they became partners to the grand scheme of her homecoming. Emily was grateful for their renewed bond, praying that Maria would find relief in knowing her family had stayed united.

They presented Sofia as the daughter of one of Emily's college friends, with the flat as a graduation gift. To cover maintenance costs, one room was leased, which Emily arranged for Maria. Sofia was portrayed as aware of Maria's condition and offered to assist with her daily and medical needs under Emily's remote supervision. Sofia also accompanied Maria monthly to see Dr. Giselle Bartonto, a Seattle occupational therapist and Emily's college colleague, for an additional caregiver fee.

"Do you think this will work? Won't she be suspicious? I worry we might scare Maria again," her husband had asked initially. "I'm sure Sofia can pull this off for her mom. She's the best person for this," Emily had replied confidently.

Maria was immediately charmed by the flat. "Oh, Emily, the apartment is perfect. The bedroom's color scheme is so relaxing. What a cozy space! And I love the kitchen—so handsome and modern. Sofia said I could use it. I love it here already, Emily. How can I thank you for always looking out for me?" Maria told Emily. "And Sofia? Whose daughter is she again? You said her mother was your college friend. So I should know her, right? She's such a fine young lady, Emily. I can't explain it, but when I saw her at the airport with your friend Lamberto, something jolted in my heart. Like I know her from somewhere. I must have met her mother before. Oh well, in time, I'll remember," Maria shared. Emily knew their plan was working.

Sofia played the role of a loving, doting caregiver, to which Maria responded warmly. Sofia introduced Maria to Seattle life, taking her to cherished locations from their past. She shared stories and myths Maria had taught her about Seattle's attractions, reversing their roles as teacher and student. Sofia found herself resonating everything back to her mother.

They regularly walked along Waterfront Park, admiring Puget Sound and the Olympic Mountains. Maria was repeatedly awed by the Seattle Aquarium and they went back to it several times. They laughed together atop the Seattle Great Wheel like "old besties".

Maria loved returning to Seattle Center Park during weekend events, reconnecting with what she called "the Seattle community I missed." She was so touched when Sofia created a collage album of their visits to the Space Needle and Chihuly Garden. Touching the photos, Maria whispered, "We could pass as mother and child, Sofia. Only I'm like the child." Sofia held back tears when she overheard it, her heart full of emotion.

They dined out often, exploring restaurants along the pathways connecting Seattle Downtown and Pike Place Market. "You said I grew up here in Seattle, Emily? I believe you now. Everywhere Sofia takes me, I feel a strong connection, even if I don't remember. But I see them differently now, more special, because of Sofia. She's such a great tour guide. I love her, Emily," Maria told her cousin nightly, unaware of Emily's silent tears of joy across the other side of the world.

Sofia tested Maria's memory with activities like cooking, requesting dishes Maria used to make, such as Pâtes d'Alsace, Ratatouille, and her Spaghetti Bolognese. "This is so yummy, Maria. Are you sure you just learned this online?" Sofia teased. "Oh, yeah, just checked online, as you said. But I think I have my personal touch. It came naturally, like I've been serving them my whole life. Served like a pro, huh?" Maria mused.

Their bond deepened. One evening, while sharing wine, Maria joked, "I can't remember any best friend I ever had, Sofia. Technically, you're the first best friend I've known. Is that okay with you?"

"Of course, Maria. You don't know how happy that makes me. I'll always be your best friend. Promise!" Sofia said, offering a handshake. But Maria pulled her close into a long hug. That night, Sofia cried, whispering, "Mom, you don't remember yet, but you're my first best friend, too. I love you so much."

They enjoyed job-hunting together. Sofia created Maria's resume, coached her for interviews, and celebrated job offers with "girls' nights out." Maria was hesitant about most offers, which Sofia respected. But when Maria was offered a job at Suzzallo Library, she was thrilled. "This is an enchanting place. I want to work here, Sofia. Will you help me?" she exclaimed. Her acceptance was a cause for celebration.

Then, mother and daughter established together Maria's work routine. Mornings began with a walk to Café de Amor, which was just few blocks away from the flat. Sofia encouraged the walk, and Maria grew close to the café's crew, especially Lamberto. She raved to Emily about the café's French-inspired interior and how everything at Café de Amor connected to her. "Goodness, cousin! Lamberto's shop is amazing! I feel transported to France every day. They have mini-talk shops where I connect with patrons. I've grown close to some, and they share their secrets with me," she said. Emily was overjoyed, seeing Maria return to her love of coaching. "It's good to be trusted again, Emily. It's rewarding when they seek my advice. Even if I wake up blank, I end each day grateful, filled with my new friends' stories. I feel my self-worth again," Maria shared.

Suddenly, Sofia was pulled from her reverie by the sound of Maria's keys at the door. "Auntie Emily, I have to go. She's home now," she said quickly. "Alright, go. I'll call your mom later. Let her settle in," Emily replied. "Yes, I promise not to mention you bugging me about running off to California," Sofia teased. "Very funny! But hold on, Sofia," Emily said, pausing. "Please call your father. Whatever you decide, whatever's in your heart, let him know. Open up to him. Lamberto misses his children, too." Sofia smiled and promised, "Of course, I will, Auntie. Thank you for everything."

"Hello! Sofia, are you home?" Maria called from the door. "Never left, Maria. I'm here!" Sofia replied, putting down the phone.

* * *

The Gift is Love
Worth Fighting For

On a regular fall day in October, Nicholas sat nervously in Maria's favorite "chat room" at Café de Amor, waiting. The clouds outside were heavy and gray, foreboding the day with Seattle's usual drizzle. Yet this did not stop Nicholas from arriving an hour earlier than his agreed meeting time with Maria. Clearly fidgety, Jasmin handed him his coffee and reminded him to relax. It was Jasmin who had told Nicholas the night before that Dr. Emily Lemaire-Dubois, Maria's cousin, wanted to have a chat with him. Emily had flown in from Paris nearly two weeks ago, when Maria was rushed to Harborview Medical Center—unconscious. Eager to know how he could help, Nicholas immediately dialed Emily's number. From her, he learned the answers to many of the questions he and the Café crew had been wondering about.

"Where is Maria? Why isn't she coming in anymore?" one crew member asked.

"Yeah, I've been getting the same questions from our regulars. Did she leave Seattle already? Does anyone know what happened to her?" another pondered aloud.

"That guy who's been coached by Maria for over a week said he even went to Suzzallo Library yesterday, hoping to talk to her, but he learned she hasn't been going to work either," someone added.

"Oh my! I hope Maria is okay. She's like a mother to us. The shop isn't the same without her—it's been more than a week," another shared with genuine sadness.

"Lamberto and Roy are mum about all of this. They said they're waiting for news too. But I know our big boss, Lamberto, is in a mess. Look at the dark circles under his eyes. Ricardo's been following him around, looking after the big guy. He's afraid Lamberto might forsake himself worrying about Maria," one of the senior baristas shared.

"Poor Lamberto. He's been waiting for so long. Well, they all have—her family too. I hope he doesn't give up now," another senior crew member said empathetically.

Hearing all this, Roy approached his crew and coached gently, "Hey, guys, we make the best coffee here while

Lamberto takes care of the rest, okay? If we want to be part of all this, let's keep making coffee that satisfies our customers. Stop the tittle-tattle for now. I know we're all concerned, but let's hope for the best and keep Lamberto's business running, all right? Go back to your stations, please. Love you, people." Though he wanted to shed light on things, Roy was as clueless as everyone else. "Thank you for your usual cooperation," he added. He knew his crew and their regular patrons shared the same fear and anxiety over Maria's absence. They were like a second family to each other at Café de Amor. "Maria, wherever you are, please know we're all waiting for you," Roy thought silently.

The night before, Emily had updated Nicholas about what had truly happened to Maria and her current condition. She explained that Sofia had heard a crash in Maria's room late at night. When she ran in, she found her mother unconscious on her bed, with a book lying on the floor—the sound of the book hitting the ground had alarmed her. Because of that, Sofia was able to rush Maria to the hospital and notify the family. After more than a week, Maria woke up from her coma—but with miraculous news. Her physicians told Emily that Maria seemed to have regained some of her memories, and with regular therapy, they believed she was on her way to full recovery.

However, Maria opted to stay in a hotel with her cousin first. "The good news is she's gathering herself together quite admirably. And Nicholas… you're the first person she wants to see," Emily revealed.

As Nicholas waited, Lamberto passed by and patted his shoulder.

"Lamberto…" Nicholas looked at him wistfully.

Lamberto slowly shook his head. "I don't know, Nicky. I really don't. Just be calm—let her take the lead."

When Maria finally opened the door of Café de Amor, it felt as if an angel had entered the room. Everyone turned toward her, frozen in awe. For several moments, baristas and regulars alike watched in silence as she walked slowly toward *Le Comptoir*, wearing her signature purple coat and scarf. Roy, slightly shaken, broke the silence with a cheerful whistle.

"Hey, Maria's in the house, people! We're so glad to see you, Maria! Is it your usual today?" he asked, trying to sound casual.

"Yes, Roy, please. I've missed my mocha," she replied softly.

"Hi, Maria!" "How are you, Maria?" "You're looking great!" "Happy to see you, my friend!" voices echoed across the café. Maria smiled warmly at each greeting.

Though shaken herself by what seemed like an "awesome apparition," Jasmin handed Maria her coffee, trying to remain composed.

"Thank you, Jasmin," Maria whispered, giving her a knowing smile, as if to say, *I know what you did.*

Nicholas stood and pulled out her chair. As Maria sat down, she looked around but didn't see Lamberto. Nicholas knew he was hiding in the locker room, overwhelmed with emotion. Understanding the turmoil Lamberto must have been feeling, Nicholas volunteered to take his place, ensuring Maria was seated comfortably—a gesture Lamberto used to offer her before.

"Good day, Nicholas. How are you doing?" Maria greeted him.

"I'm doing well, Coach. We missed you..." His voice trembled as emotion broke through. "I'm sorry, Maria. I never meant to hurt you. I didn't want to bring back your pain. Please believe me—you've inspired me. You're the only person who gave me the courage to..." His voice trailed off.

"You mean this, Nicholas? To do *this?*" Maria said, pulling out a package wrapped in violet gloss paper with a golden bow. It was the "gift" he had sent her before she fell ill.

Nicholas was speechless, tears streaming down his face.

Maria chuckled softly. "Oh, come on, Nicholas. Dry those tears—they don't match your business suit." Her humor broke the tension, and Nicholas laughed as he wiped his eyes. It was always Maria's style to calm and comfort with ease.

"Nicholas, you did it. You wrote your first book, my friend. You finally gave birth to the writer the world has been waiting for," she said with a wink. "So, I'm not here to be your 'Coach,' Nicky. I was never one. I always told you that, right? I'm just a friend who believes in you—and who waited for you to believe in yourself, too. There's nothing more fulfilling for me than seeing you and everyone here at Café de Amor shine." She paused, lost briefly in thought. Then, looking straight at him, she continued, "And Nicky, you just had your shining moment. This is a shimmering gift." She raised the book written by Nicholas. "A glittering package, Nicky. So brilliant that when I opened it, its shine blinded me at first. But your words sparkled like gems, illuminating my path."

With a motherly smile, she added, "Now don't talk much, Nicky. I asked you here because I want you to listen to me this time. I want you to hear, straight from me, how proud I am of you." She smiled again—the same smile that always left Nicholas breathless.

Maria opened the book, her slender fingers touching every word as she read:

He drove down the streets of Seattle, thinking of her all the time…

He would go to the church

Recalling the days, he watched his mother cried before the altar

Venting out the burdens in her heart.

"What is wrong, Mom? Why are you crying?" he often asked

"Nothing, my son," was how she shielded him from what was tearing

her apart

"I may be young. But I will understand and help, Mom"

If you just tell me…please," he begged her all the time

"This is nothing, my dear. Always remember to **pray***, son*

Even if Mommy is into something, there is nothing I cannot take

Just pray and stay as my adorable, loving boy.

Would you?" she assured him

For many years now, he wondered…"I hope I have kept my promise

To make you smile, Mom. Every day, as long as you want me to,

I will be your clown. I will make you laugh…

Oh, how I miss your laughter! I will drive you nuts with happiness…"

"My boy, Zachary. He was so young, Nicholas, when I left him. I think he was just in high school. I regret I missed his growing up years. However, my heart is over-joyed that he grew up strong, mature. He was not robbed off with his innocence and hope. I thank God I left him with something lasting and durable…" Maria reflected on.

"How can I missed the signs if I was your best-friend, Mom?

Did I fail you?" she often blamed herself

"When I had school problems, you helped me fix them up

When I lost friends, you stayed, and just hugged me closely

When I had my first love, you taught me to trust but be strong

However, at the times of your personal unrest, where am I?

I thought technology would keep us close wherever I may be

However, I was wrong and missed the signs.

I should never have left Seattle

Now, I will hold your hand. I will walk you through these dark days

I will watch over you while you are asleep…

I will be here, Mom. I will be your friend…"

"Of course, my Sofia! My strong-willed, independent Sofia," she gave in to those heavy tears. "Do you know, Nicholas, that she is my biggest first? Everything I learned about parenting, I first learned from her," she laughed out heartily. "We had so much ups and downs, mother and daughter. You see, I lost my own parents quite early. I raised Sofia based on the warm memories of my own mother. It was not easy for a new Mom to piece together "the how to's" of raising a child until one experiences it along the way with her own child. Thus, I would say, my first-born taught me a lot that I was already a better Mom when Zachary came. They were five years apart," she admitted with a loud chuckle. "And, for the second time, it is unimaginable how my Sofia opened me up again to a brand new world. It is incredible to be a mother, Nicky! How a mother's struggles can turn into her children's beacon light and make it all worth it. Sofia has grown exactly to the woman I dreamt her to be. She did not fail me at all," Maria exclaimed; one cannot miss euphoria and pride in her voice.

We are sisters from different mothers

Separated by time and space

Propelled by dreams apart

But with the same blood flowing in our veins

No mountains… or seas can stop me from saving you

I will rescue you, sister

"Emily… she has always been my rock. Indeed, family is family wherever our lives take us to. We will always have each other's back, through thick or thin," Maria smiled; so grateful of the remaining kin from her bloodline.

"Cappuccino, Americano, Hot Mocha… on their way

Grab some croissant? Empanada, Madame?"

The hustle and bustle inside this world exhilarate you

It is like seeing Paris in a romantic scene

One that you would watch over and over again

"No doubt, every morning, you keep watch of them all"

Immerse yourself into the songs of their souls

Giving much of your time and kindness

Basking into their stories and dreams that come true

However, when you put them all together,

At the palm of your gracious hand

You picture the blood and sweat of a familiar love

One that turned all these to reality

Waiting… longing… begging from afar

The sacrificing one…

The enduring one…

The everlasting love…

(Maria went through the excerpts from Nicholas's book—about love, family, and reflection—culminating in Maria's heartfelt memories of the people she loves and the learning she had about motherhood, resilience, and love.)

When she finished reading, she looked at Nicholas and asked, "Do you think it's worth fighting for, Nicholas?"

"I strongly do, Maria. I witnessed it all. Your love story is inspiring," he replied, placing a hand over his heart.

"Thank you for your courage. Nobody else would have dared—but you, my friend. You're heaven-sent," Maria said with a cheerful toss of her cup.

"Please don't forget," Nicholas replied with a grin, "I wouldn't have had the courage without you, Maria. One great coach once told me to follow my heart—and there, I would find my muse. I certainly did. Thank you, Coach… and friend. Welcome back to Café de Amor. We all love you here."

"Oh, I love you all more!" Maria exclaimed loudly, so everyone could hear. Roy and the Café crew joined in, echoing, "Love you, too, Maria!" The café filled with laughter and warmth, a perfect contrast to the gray drizzle outside.

In the locker room, Lamberto heard the joyful noise filling his shop. He bowed his head and wept quietly.

Nicholas pulled out Maria's chair again as she prepared to leave.

"Nicholas?" she said, pausing. "Promise me this is just the first of your many books, okay? And by the way—I love the title. Nothing could have been better. What a perfect choice." She patted his shoulder, waved to everyone, and smiled as she said, "Enjoy your coffee! See you all tomorrow here at Café de Amor."

Behind her, Nicholas whispered repeatedly to himself the title of his gift to the world— Nicholas Novac's first book ever:

"Love Worth Fighting For."

* * *

Autumn's Surprise

"Sleep tight, sister. I am going for an early walk," Maria whispered to Emily and touched her head lightly.

"What? Maria? Is it not too early for a walk?" Emily muttered under the white sheet of her comfortable bed at Edgewater Hotel in downtown Seattle. Both cousins had been staying in the said hotel for two weeks already since Maria's release from the hospital. To Emily's great relief, Maria had been recuperating well, and they had spent all days and nights catching up and bonding with one another, just like old times. Emily had lovingly kept her promise and served as Maria's constant point, cementing the life details that connected her past and her present. Maria had been absorbing it all fervently in her heart and mind. She had finally come to terms with the truths she had unconsciously buried before. Now, with all intentions, she gradually exhumed them to marvelously mix with the promise of her future. "Do you need me to accompany you, Maria? Just wait. I will shower up and join you," Emily offered.

"No, sister. Let me do this on my own," she gave her a great, big smile. "I think I am ready for the grand homecoming I have been telling you about!" Maria exclaimed as she grabbed her coat and hurried outside their hotel room. Emily felt a little jittery but decided to let it be. She grabbed her phone from the side table, dialed Sofia's number, and leaked out with delight, "Dear niece, be ready. Go to Café de Amor. It might be happening today." She knew, deep in her heart, Maria had fully prepared herself for the moment. She was wholly ready to embrace back her once-lost world and everyone she loved in it. "They will be in for a great surprise," she said to herself. With a smile, Emily went back to her sleep, unruffled and peaceful.

Maria clearly recalled how she always loved fall—"Autumn." Each season of the year brought its individual delight, but since her childhood, autumn had been her ultimate favorite. To the north of their hotel, she followed the trail towards Elliott Bay Park and Myrtle Edwards Park, which gave her a perfect view of the Seattle Waterfront. She sat down on one of the benches, taking in the crisp air from the Pacific Ocean. Beautiful memories of the summers she spent with her children filled her mind. She recalled how her children raved over her well-prepared picnic goodies all the time, how they ran around or went biking while she watched after them, and how she read them stories as they took "siesta," short naps under the sun after a good play. Her heart skipped a beat when she caught a good glimpse of the Great Wheel from afar. She closed her eyes and smiled sweetly as she reminisced about that romantic night which totally changed her young life—the night when Lamberto popped the big question, "Will you be my wife?" under the starry skies on top of the giant Ferris wheel— and she said, "Yes!"

As she took her steps towards Café de Amor, right in the middle of downtown Seattle, Maria appreciated how the city never lacked the lushness of green. That is why, historically, Seattle is nicknamed the "Emerald City" due to its abundant greenery and parks. Seattle always boasted various kinds of pine trees, with all their shades of green and fresh pine scents. All year round, these Seattle pine trees, like endless Christmas trees, would stand mighty and proud. Yet, just like every fall, Maria's eyes feasted on the wonderful colors of fallen leaves on the ground, and she enjoyed such a morning picturesque. She remembered a poem she once wrote:

Music of fall

What a feast to see!

Yellow, orange, red, and green

All the colors burst for thrill

And when the leaves fall

One hears… crunch

Crunch, crunch, crunch

Every step is music to the ears!

Though each fall may be hard

But true joy stays up and down

Such unending circle of life

Keeps the rhythm in our hearts

Maria mused that she was, indeed, thrilled with the Paris lifestyle. She would forever be indebted to the Dubois family for taking her in during her temporary affliction. Being immersed in Paris was like opening up blank pages of a new "life journal" filled with glamour and elegance. For Maria, the simple pleasures of Paris, meshed with the city's famous cultural refinement, were just unbelievably amazing to experience. "It was a respite I deserved—beautiful enough to make me forget for a while, but powerful as well to pull me back to my feet," she contemplated. "In anyone's lifetime, one must learn the significance of moments when a stop, a reroute, or a recharge is needed. A hiatus to connect with one's core is crucial in living. A worthy pause from all the world's craziness should never be a reason for guilt. Life also mandates self-care," she declared. "One cannot love fully if one's cup is lacking." Thus, she promised herself that, aside from Paris, she would continuously gift herself the opportunities to travel and explore more—not just of places, but of self-discovery.

Moreover, as all her memories rose to the surface, Maria grasped vividly that, among the many cities she experienced, "Seattle is home." Everything she held deeply in her heart—people, places, memories—were real in this "Rain City." "Home is an important constant in one's life. It has to be kept strong at all times," she deduced. "But home takes various forms in different stages of a person's life. At one point, it could be a place for rejuvenation. Nevertheless, it could also be a person or a group who can give comfort and belongingness. Home is one's safety net—one's fallback when all else gets rough. Everything else may fade, but hopefully not home. Not again..." she repeated to herself. Maria loved everything about her home —its mild, temperate climate, its popular coffee culture, its mix of urban look and rural feel, and its laid-back serenity against the hustle and bustle of other cities of the world. Most of all, her home went back to the beautiful people she shared memories with. "This is where I was born and raised. This is where my love is. This is my place in the world." And she could not be happier than ever.

Weather forecasters shared that approximately 226 days of the year, Seattle is covered in heavy clouds. That is why the city is also described on the web as "The Gray City." Expecting a drizzle of rain at some point in the day is common; thus, everyone goes out with a hood in handy. "Walking under the rain" is one of the many pleasures, too. However, when you hear people say, "The sun is out today!" it is a declaration that it will be a rare, beautiful day—an open invitation to do something different. To Maria, that day would definitely be unforgettable.

She opened the door of Café de Amor, and the familiar aroma engulfed her. "It is a taste of Paris in my own home," she proudly told herself. She could not be more at home when the usual greetings sounded off around the shop. "Hello, Maria! You have a minute later?" "Hey, Coach, things turned out well for me yesterday. Thanks!" "Oh, Maria! All's good with me now. Thanks for listening…" Everything in Café de Amor, including all the people she connected with, reaffirmed who she had become and what she truly wanted to be. Everything in Café de Amor represented dreams that used to be so abstract, far, and unattainable for her. Even the dreams she had failed to recognize creeping in her soul were now encapsulated into one breathtaking structure, built from the foundation of faith and love. "Dreams do come true," she took in with great pride, then added, "Faith and grit can make them all happen," amused by Lamberto's accomplishment with Café de Amor. However, in deeper retrospection, "Distance brought me and Lamberto apart. It is one of the many tests of time. Despite that, Lamberto always knew my soul even from afar. How could I have ever doubted him?" she acknowledged her frailty and basked in the gratefulness of a love that never actually left her side, even when tested in fire—a testament that love is beyond space and time.

After she spent her morning pleasantries with Roy, and while waiting for her mocha to be handed to her, Maria thoroughly observed the customers in the shop. There were new faces now, probably intrigued by the growing popularity of Café de Amor and checking it out for themselves. Maria looked forward to getting to know them all more someday. However, tranquility rested more on her as she watched the faces of those she had come to know deeply through the years—Nicholas and many others—those whose stories of struggles and successes she had listened to and, somehow, became part of. "How can we be so absorbed with our own miseries? How can we allow ourselves to be drowned by fleeting loneliness?" she reflected. "If, despite our struggles, we just manage to open up and accept that we are not alone; if we can keep on trusting and reaching out; if we stay humble and never stop believing in the beauty and kindness of others— probably, we will never lose ourselves," she declared to herself.

"If we always answer back with kindness, allowing it to hold us all together, wouldn't this be a better world? If we touch others with a grateful heart, wouldn't life seem lighter? If this becomes our inspiration every day, wouldn't that be a noble passion to live for?" she pondered further. Right there and then, she understood that beyond her familial duties, which she would forever honor, she, too, had a greater calling to the community.

Greg, one of her client-friends, requested to chat with her in one of the rooms about the community project he had previously consulted her on. Maria joined him, and as usual, Lamberto pulled the chair for her. She smiled at him longingly.

Greg shared how his group had progressed so far. Sadly, though, his members were beginning to raise differing agendas. Maria assured Greg it was a normal hiccup in any group undertaking. "It is not something unsurmountable," she cheered up his dwindling spirit. "Actually, it is during trying times that your leadership is truly tested, Greg. So, hang in there. Remember, a leader's strength is not measured when things are smooth sailing," she teased him with the thought. "It is when you lead them rowing in synchrony, even during the disturbing tides. Leadership is about communicating a common vision—constantly guiding and inspiring them to believe in it. The question is, how will you do that?" Maria challenged him to think through his predicament. Immediately, Greg lit up with several plans. Maria nodded approvingly as she sensed his renewed enthusiasm. Wrapping it up, she said, "Those are all brilliant, Greg, and, by the way, why don't you invite your members here? Have coffee with them and listen to what they think about your unity plan. I will join in if you like," she offered. "Open your mind to how they will react and respond, Greg. That is what a leader does—listen to them. Then, recalibrate your goals with them. Are you comfortable with that?" she asked. "Yeah, yeah, that is a lovely idea, Maria. I think I am up for it. Thank you, as always," Greg excitedly agreed. "Perfect, Greg! See you all in Café de Amor," she said, raising her mug for a cheer.

Lamberto approached and pulled her chair. "Maria, your ride is here." Maria abruptly stood up, feeling her heart jolt with joy. She curtsied at Greg so fast, patted Lamberto's arm, and ran outside the shop so quickly that everyone was a bit shocked by such a rush. They could not help but follow her sudden dash.

Outside, Zachary was standing, resting on the side hood of his blue sedan in front of Café de Amor. He saw Maria dashing, and before he could even utter her name, she had already reached him and started touching his wavy hair, his broad shoulders, his cheeks, as if she was reacquainting her touch with his features. He felt awkward and tried to move away from her with a slight push. However, he saw tears flowing down her cheeks. Jokingly, he said, "Oh wait, wait, you missed me,

Madame'? Putting his hands in front of him, aiming to halt Maria's movements, he stammered, "Ahh, ahh, Madame' Maria, what is up with you? Wait, please. Hold on, please, Madame'?"

"Oh, aren't you such a hard-to-get, my Zachary boy?" Maria laughed and joked loudly.

Zachary froze, dumbfounded. "What did you say? Zachary boy?" he looked at her questioningly. "Yes, my dear, you are my one and only Zachary boy, are you not?" Maria smiled calmly, though tears continuously flowed down her cheeks.

Zachary held his breath, collected his thoughts, and knew there was only one person in this world who used that endearment for him. He held her stare this time and whispered, "Mom...?"

"Yes, Zachary! Yes, this is Mom!" Maria let it out. This time, Zachary broke down completely—a picture of a six-foot man, burying his head on the feeble shoulder of Maria, releasing all the heavy burdens he had been holding up for so long. He cried explosively; his shoulders quivered; his moans so heavy, one understood there were so many words he wanted to utter, but none came out—just a wail of unexplainable happiness. Maria consoled him lovingly, "It is okay. I am here now. I am sorry, but I will make it up to you, my son." And every time she whispered those words, he moaned louder, quivered more, and Maria held him closer to her bosom, just like in the memories of his younger days when he came home from a petty fight or fell from his bike.

"Mom…"—a soft whisper from behind them. Maria stayed hugging Zachary but slightly turned around to open her other arm for Sofia. She knew that voice even from a thousand miles away. And Sofia rushed to them, shouting, "Mom!" All three hugged, cuddled, and clutched each other's bodies as if forbidding even the tiniest space between them to separate them again. For a standstill of several minutes, mother and children did not separate, but they exchanged laughter and giggles in between cries for their long years of unleased heartaches.

Inside Café de Amor, everyone stood still, watching the movie-like scene outside. Their mouths opened in disbelief; others pursed their lips to prevent trembling, while some squeezed each other's hands for comfort. For anyone who had followed the family's story and had been in cahoots with its secrecy, they also felt tremendous relief and liberation. It was the most heartwarming moment at Café de Amor.

"You did it, Nicky. I am so proud of you," Jasmin whispered to Nicholas and kissed his cheek. Nicholas, slightly taken aback but glad for it, replied, "It is nothing without your help, Jasmin. Thank you for trusting me. And let me tell you this—next time, the story is about you," he reached out for her hand. "You are my next muse. And my perfect love."

"Love is in the air, people!" Roy shouted out. Then, everyone clapped, sang, and danced around the shop.

But in the middle of it all, Lamberto stood transfixed. "Should I join them? Should I hold back? Does she want me, too? Is this really happening at all?" There were myriads of thoughts running endlessly in his head.

"Lamberto, should you not be doing something now?" Ricardo badgered his friend. Lamberto just stayed motionless, spellbound by the scene.

Recovering from their dramatic reunion, Zachary motioned to Maria that she would be late for work. "Let us drive to Suzzallo now, Mom," he joyfully reminded her. "Oh yeah! Thank you, son." Then, addressing both, "But we will have a dinner celebration tonight, okay? What do you want? Would you like your Ratatouille?" she teased, pinching Zachary's nose. "Yes! Ratatouille all the way!" Zachary hollered with both hands raised in victory. Sofia laughed at him and bade her mother a good luck kiss.

Maria held her back a little longer, cupping her cheeks with both hands, and said, "Thank you for all you did, Sofia. Now, it is time for your dreams, my child." Excitedly, "Even if the dream is in California, Mom?" Sofia opened up. "Oh goodness, daughter! The world is yours for the taking. Wherever it may lead us, I will be with you, dear," Maria said, and they rested their heads together, smiling and crying together. "But wait, children, I need to do one last thing," she winked at Zachary and Sofia, then sprinted back to the shop.

Panting a little, "Lamberto?" Maria asked straight away because she immediately saw him standing in the middle of the shop while everybody was dancing around him. "I was just thinking…" pausing a little with caution. "I have listened to almost everyone's story in this room. But I have never heard yours?" Maria started to take slow strides toward Lamberto. All dropped what they were doing again and just stood watching the couple, savoring every detail of what was to happen next.

"Would you like to have dinner tonight and tell me your story this time? Ahh, with the children?" she paused again, then declared, "Do you know that I make the best Ratatouille in town?" and gave him her cutest smile.

"I know you do," Lamberto answered in a soft, stammering whisper.

"So, would you be there… this time?" Maria shyly asked.

"I will never miss it for the world… this time, Maria," Lamberto softly answered back, still in a hypnotic daze.

With that, Maria touched his chest, stooped a little to brush his cheek with a shy kiss. Then, like a teenager, she turned around cheerfully and shouted, "See you tonight, my love!" And to her amused audience, who she knew were transfixed by her daring action, she called out, "See you in Café de Amor tomorrow, everyone!" From outside, Lamberto saw his children waving happily at him.

"So, what do you say now, amigo?" Ricardo teased and danced while everyone clapped continuously.

All Lamberto could say was, "Free… Coffee is free… Coffee is on me today," slowly waking up from his trance.

* * *

About the Author

Roxanne Vasquez is a Human Resources professional with extensive experience in both the public and private sectors. Before relocating to the United States in 2017, she established a successful career in the Philippines as an HR executive and Certified Performance Coach. With a master's degree in Public Administration (major in Organizational Studies), Roxanne now lends her expertise to non-profit organizations in Washington State. Through her writing, she advocates for human transformational development, inspiring individuals to fulfil their highest potential.

For queries and comments about the book and author, send email to thecoachcafe1@gmail.com

9 781970 846126